Billionaire Seeks An Heir: Unplanned Fair Tale

Misha Carver

Billionaire Seeks An Heir: Unplanned Fair Tale

Copyright © 2015 by Misha Carver

ISBN 978-1988343112

This book is dedicated to four very important people in my life. To my children who stood by me and encouraged me every step of the way even when I wasn't feeling very creative. I love you with all my heart. You all are the best cheerleaders ever!

Acknowledgments

No book is the effort of just one person, and this is no exception. Every writer has a team, even if it's not official.

I would like to thank:

Claudette Cruz, The Editing Sweetheart, for painstakingly putting up with my incessant use of commas and tirelessly going over my work with a fine tooth comb.

Jacqueline Sweet for putting up with my vagueness and indecision and coming up with a magnificent cover for this series.

My wonderful readers, many of whom I've had the chance to interact with over social media. A book is nothing but paper with words on it without someone to read it. Thank you for taking the time to read the words I've written and for believing in me.

Table of Contents

Chapter 1 ~ Jason

"**Y**OU'RE SO LUCKY," BOB said as he swallowed back his beer. "You don't have anyone to tell you when to come home. The only one who calls the shots is you."

"Ah, but that's where you're wrong, my friend," I said as I carefully aimed my cue and took my shot. "I'd give anything to have someone sitting there waiting for me when I get home. Instead, all I have is Rufus."

"At least Rufus doesn't argue," Jacob laughed, setting down his glass of wine while he got ready to take his shot.

"Or make you sleep on the couch," Bob cut in.

"Have you ever seen how much room that dog takes up on the bed?" I said. "The way he sprawls out there's barely any room left for me."

"Look at it this way," Bob said as he put his arm around my shoulder. "You've got the best of both worlds. You aren't nailed down to any one woman, and you get to keep all of your money to yourself. No woman can take you for half of it if things don't work out. Stay a bachelor, man. Marriage is hell."

"Guys, I get where you're all coming from. But I'll turn 35 years old this year. I've been taking an inventory of my life, and of everything I have. It's all just possessions. It means nothing if I have no one to share it all with," I said as I chalked up my cue.

"What's got into you, man?" Bob said with a concerned look on his face.

"Yeah, has the eternal bachelor gone soft on us?" Jacob said as he raised his eyebrow.

"It's just that I'm realizing that if I died tomorrow, I have no heir to carry on my family name, or to run my business. I have no one to leave anything to. What does it all mean, if you don't have a legacy to leave behind for someone to inherit?"

"Either I've had too much beer, or that's the deepest thing I've ever heard," Jacob said.

"Have another beer, buddy," Bob said. "And Jason, maybe you should too. You're going all flaky on us."

"No guys, I'm serious. I'm at a point where I want someone to share my life with, and I want an heir to pass it all on to."

The waitress came around to collect our empty bottles and glasses. I threw her some cash and ordered another round. I loved Friday nights out with the guys. I could relax in freedom in the back of Sparky's Bar and Poolroom without anyone recognizing me while we solved the world's problems, or at least our own.

"You know that's not going to be easy, man," Bob said. "Look at all the women that throw themselves at your feet now, all opportunists. You'll be hard pressed to find someone who's not just out to get their hands on your money."

"What he needs," Jacob said, "is to find someone who's as successful as he is. It doesn't matter what field she's in, as long as she has a similar net worth."

"So what am I supposed to do?" I asked. "Ask women for their bank statements as a prerequisite for a first date?"

"Well, it might rule a lot of people out," Jacob said.

"Yeah, but he might also scare a lot of good candidates away that don't want to share that information so early on. Besides, in the interest of full disclosure, if he's going to make them share, he should have to do it as well. I doubt that he plans on doing that," Bob added.

"That's a good point," Jacob said. "Aren't there billionaire dating agencies or something for stinking rich people like you?"

"Yeah," I laughed. "With women whose profiles are nothing but lies. I tried that once. I'm never going back."

"What about treating it like a job?" Bob asked.

"Are you saying being married to me would be a full-time job?" I laughed.

"No. I'm just saying, what about interviewing people and finding out who you like. Then pick a couple from the pool to date, and find your perfect match from there."

"It feels too much like a reality show for me," I said as I curled up my nose at the idea.

"Well, it's not like you're going to advertise it, like who wants to marry a millionaire..."

"Billionaire, at least get it right," I chuckled.

"And let's not forget arrogant," Jacob added. "Seriously though, it's not a bad idea. Get women to audition, or rather interview, for the job. You could call them back for second and third interviews. It's perfect."

"I don't know. It sounds sneaky and underhanded."

"Gold diggers and opportunists are sneaky and underhanded," Bob reminded me.

"I guess when you put it that way, it's not that terrible of an idea. Besides, I'm only protecting my assets."

"Exactly," Jacob said. "Protect your own ass and make sure you find the perfect woman for the job. Maybe none of them will qualify, or maybe you'll wind up with a few of them to choose from. You'll never know until you try."

"Well, that's it for me, boys. I have an early morning tomorrow," I said as I grabbed my sweater off the back of my chair.

"Tomorrow? Tomorrow's Saturday," Bob said questioningly.

"Yeah, well, the boss's work is never done," I said with a smile. "Have a good one, guys."

"At least think about it," Jacob said.

"I will," I lied. I never intended to give it another thought. Interviewing potential wives was the stupidest idea I'd ever heard of.

When I got home I gave my maid the rest of the night off and immediately flopped down on the couch. As I flipped through the television channels, I must have fallen asleep. I woke up the next morning to the sounds of the birds singing, still wearing my clothes from the bar the night before.

I scrambled to get ready to head down to the office. Ratings sweeps had just ended, and we were debating which television shows to cancel and which to renew for another season. I hated working Saturdays, but during sweeps, sometimes it couldn't be helped, especially during negotiations.

When I arrived at the office, my secretary, Julie, greeted me with a hot cup of coffee as she'd done every morning for the past five years. I didn't know what I'd do without her. She knew exactly what I liked and she always delivered.

"Hey Julie," I said. "Can I see you in my office for a second?"

"Coming, Mr. Donnelly," she said.

"I'm going to ask you to do something rather strange," I said as I folded my hands on my desk.

"Fire away," she said with her spunky little attitude.

"I want to have a baby, and I'm in the market for a wife. I want you to set up interviews with women for me."

"So, you want me to be your personal dating service?" she asked with a huge grin on her face.

"Not quite. I just want you to prequalify people before I meet them. I'm trying to steer clear of the gold diggers. I want someone who loves me for me, not for my money."

"Ah, so no more one-night stands for the lone Jason Donnelly. New York's most eligible bachelor is about to marry himself off, I take it."

"Enough of the snide remarks, Julie. I'm counting on you. Just do it," I said exhausted.

"Consider it done," she said as she gave me a sly grin and walked out of my office.

"SO, WHAT EXACTLY WAS your interview for?" my roommate Liz asked.

"Public relations intern at Donnelly Multimedia. I won't get the job. I just don't have the experience," I said as I flopped down on the couch with a bag of potato chips.

"Not with an attitude like that, you won't. You need to throw your shoulders back, get that chin up, and show the world the Jerrica Rollins that I know. The one that can conquer the world." She knocked everything off the stand beside her as she flung her arms around in the air.

"I just finished school, Liz. I don't have the background to get a position like that. There is no way in the world they're going to hire me."

"How did the interview go?"

"It seemed okay," I said as I washed down my chips with some soda. "I was in and out in ten minutes, though. That's how I know I didn't get it."

"Stay positive, you never know," she said as she got up to answer the phone. "Jerrica," she said as she held her hand over the receiver. "It's for you. It's Donnelly Multimedia."

My eyes were as big as saucers and my jaw dropped to the floor the second she said it. I couldn't believe they actually called.

Then, as I reached out to grab the receiver, I realized there was only one reason they would call back this soon after the interview. To tell me I didn't get the job. I swallowed what I had in my mouth quickly before answering.

"Hello. Yes, this Jerrica Rollins. Okay. Yes. Thanks for calling."

"Well..." Liz said as she stood across the room waiting for the verdict.

I looked at the floor with a dismal expression on my face. "They just called to tell me...that I got the job," I said excitedly. "I start Monday morning at nine a.m. sharp."

"Oh my God, I'm so happy for you," Liz squealed as she threw her arms around me.

"I can't believe it," I said. "I didn't think I'd get it in a million years."

"Get dressed," she said. "We're going out to celebrate. My treat."

"Where do you want to go?" I asked.

"I don't know, it's Friday night. A bar I guess."

"Hey, do you want to play some pool?" I asked. "I haven't done that in so long."

"Sure, why not? I used to love playing billiards."

"Why don't we just go in what we've got on, then," I said, looking down at my faded jeans and comfy sweatshirt. I really didn't feel like getting all dolled up when I was already settled in for a quiet night at home.

"Nope. I'll have none of that. We're going to get ourselves all done up for a night on the town. Now go make yourself gorgeous before we go rack up some balls."

It figured that she'd want to get dressed up. So much for my quiet night on the couch. It was really sweet of her to take me out to celebrate though, and I wanted to humor her. Besides, I was ecstatic that I got the job.

Chapter 3 ~ Jason

"YOU STARTED INTERVIEWING WIVES yet?" Bob asked as the waitress dropped a pitcher of beer off at our table.

"God no. I'm leaving the first interview up to my secretary. I'll take it from there. I don't have time to sit down with every candidate," I said as I took a swig from my mug.

"You don't have time to sit down and talk to someone, but you think you have time for a wife who you'll need to care for twenty-four hours a day? Now how does that make sense?" Jacob asked.

"You guys just don't understand my lifestyle," I said.

"Either that, or you need to sort out your priorities," Bob said. "So, are we just going to sit here all night, or are we going to play some pool?"

"Would you look at that," Jacob said, pointing toward the door. I turned around in my chair and saw two women walking up to the bar. They were both gorgeous. The tall one wore a black spandex dress and had long auburn hair. The petite one wore a royal blue dress that wasn't quite as snug but still flattered her curvaceous body quite nicely. Her wavy flaxen hair hung softly over her shoulders and down her back. I wanted desperately to touch it, to run my fingers through it.

"Jason...Jason," Bob said as he nudged my elbow and sent my beer flying.

"What? Sorry, did you say something?"

"I asked you if you were going to set up the balls, but apparently you had other things on your mind."

"Yeah, I guess. Right now, I need to go up to the bar and get a napkin," I said. I walked up to the bar where the two women stood. While I was waiting to get a cloth from the bartender, I figured one of them would strike up a conversation with me, but neither spoke a word.

I turned to the auburn-haired beauty hoping I'd be able to weasel my way into talking to her friend. "Busy place in here tonight," I said.

She grabbed their drinks off the bar, looked at me as if I were a parasite, rolled her eyes, and the two of them went off and found a table. I stood there feeling like a fool. No one had ever rejected me before, and I wasn't about to have any part of it.

After the bartender handed me a cloth, I asked him to send two drinks over to the table the ladies sat down at. When I went back to my table and cleaned up the mess, I watched and waited. When the waitress took the drinks over to the girls, she pointed, indicating that they were from me. The girls smiled and waved. *Ha, I've still got it,* I thought.

A few minutes later the waitress came over and sat both drinks down on our table. "The women at the other table said to tell you they don't accept drinks from men they don't know."

I bit my lip and rubbed my chin for a second. They had certainly piqued my curiosity. "Wait a second," I said to the waitress as I scribbled a note down on a napkin.

Care to join us? Then you'll know me.

"Can you take this back over to the ladies," I said. I watched as she walked back over and handed my note to the girls. They giggled as they read it, and then they promptly got up and left.

"Well, it looks like old Jason finally struck out," Jacob said.

"Shut up," I said. "And don't call me old."

"Good thing you're looking for a wife, buddy," Bob said, "because it looks like your days as a ladies' man are numbered."

I sat there shaking my head going over everything in my mind. I hadn't been rude or obnoxious. In fact, I thought I'd been downright charming. Maybe the guys were right. Maybe I was getting old.

"Tough break," the waitress said as she cleared off their table. "For what it's worth, I would have taken the drink."

"Yeah, thanks," I said.

"Whoa, Jason, you got a live one there," Bob said.

"Guys, she's cute, but I already told you, my days of one-night stands are over. I'm looking for something meaningful in my life. It wouldn't be fair to me and it wouldn't be fair to her."

After we drank some beers while I wallowed in my sorrows about getting older and getting turned down, I racked up the balls. We played a few rounds of pool, before I decided to call it quits for the night.

"Gotta go into the office again tomorrow?" Jacob asked.

"No. I'm just tired. I think I'm going to hit the sack," I said as I took some cash out of my wallet to cover the rest of their evening.

"Getting tired early on a Friday night is the first sign of getting old," he said.

"You just keep your mouth shut or I'll put that money away," I laughed as I turned around and left.

All I could think about on the drive home and while I lay in bed was the beautiful girl with the flaxen hair. Try as I might, I couldn't get her off my mind.

"COULD YOU BELIEVE THAT jerk at the bar earlier?" Liz said.

"Yeah, I know," I said as I flopped back down on our overstuffed couch in my pajamas. "I hate it when a guy just assumes he can buy me a drink. I don't want to owe anyone anything."

"I know, right. They buy you a drink and they expect a whole night of ravenous sex. What do they think we are, dollar-store hookers? If they want a night of sex, I at least want a flat screen TV," she said.

"Or a diamond necklace," I said, laughing. "Fuck expecting anything for a four-dollar drink. Men are crazy."

"You've got that right," she said as she grabbed a bottle of water out of the kitchen.

"Where are you going so bright and early?" Liz asked.

"I want to run a few errands and pick up a few things that I'll need for work on Monday," I said as I put on my earrings and grabbed my purse.

"Look at you going all career woman on me," she laughed as she flopped down on the couch in her sweats.

"Do you want to come?" I asked her.

"No. I have a date with the couch. I'm not going anywhere."

"Suit yourself then," I said as I headed out the door.

I hobbled into the coffee shop with a broken heel while I carried countless shopping bags in my arms. I had no idea shopping could be so treacherous. When I got to the counter and placed my order, I fished around trying to get into my purse to find some change before grabbing my coffee.

Relieved that I could finally get off my aching feet, I tried to balance my coffee in my hand, while I maneuvered the heavy bags over to a table. It wasn't an easy feat considering that I had to limp every step of the way.

"Damn," I said when I finally got situated in a chair and sat the bags down.

"What's the matter?" a friendly voice asked.

"Oh, it's nothing," I said. "I just broke a nail."

"Looks like you broke your heel too," he observed.

As soon as I looked up, I wished I didn't have so many bags to carry. All I wanted to do was get out of there. Standing behind the empty chair across from mine was the dark-haired stranger from the bar.

"Mind if I sit down?" he asked as he put his hand on the back of the chair. I found it rather assuming of him to think I'd be sitting in a coffee shop all by myself, even if I was.

"My friend's just grabbing her coffee," I lied as I played with my broken fingernail.

"Well, that's funny," he said, "because there's no one in line at the cash. Why don't you let me help you with that?" he said as he reached over and lightly brushed my hand with his fingers.

"Help me with what?" I asked as I looked at him and took a sip of my coffee. His steel blue eyes looked almost violet the way the light shone through the windows, and I couldn't stop staring at them.

"With your nail, silly," he laughed as he picked up my hand and inspected it closer.

"No, no," I squealed. "Don't hurt me. Don't rip it off."

"I'm not going to hurt you. I just happen to have some of this," he said as he pulled some super glue out of his briefcase. I looked at him curiously as he took the lid off and took my hand in his.

While he held my hand still, he squeezed the tube over my nail and laid a thin line of glue over the break.

"I hope we don't get bonded together," I said as he held my nail together, waiting for the glue to set. He looked away from my hand, and we stared into each other's eyes for a brief moment while we smirked.

"I'm skilled in the art of gluing," he said. "I paid attention in Kindergarten."

I watched in awe as my nail sealed back together. "Where on earth did you learn this, and how long will it hold?" I asked him.

"I grew up in a house full of girls, and until your nail grows long enough for you to cut it off without it hurting," he said. "Now, why don't you let me fix that shoe of yours while I'm at it?"

"Give it a go, Mr. Fix It," I said as I handed him my shoe. He had the heel repaired before I was finished with my coffee. "Thank you so much, Mister..."

"Call me Jason," he said as he squeezed my fingers and smiled at me.

"Thank you so much, Jason. I'm afraid I have to be going now..."

"I'm sorry, I didn't catch your name," he said, looking at me with a sly grin.

"It's Miss Rollins," I said as I stood up and started grabbing my bags.

"Okay, Miss Rollins, you have a wonderful day," he said with a puzzled look on his face.

"You too," I said as I got up and headed out of the coffee shop. I peeked around to see if he was watching me walk out, and caught him in the act. Sly little bugger didn't even buy me a coffee. If he thought a little bit of super glue was going to get him anywhere he had another thing coming.

Chapter 5 ~ Jason

MISS ROLLINS. I DIDN'T even have a first name for her, just Miss Rollins with the gorgeous blonde hair and the velvety soft hands. At least I was getting somewhere. I finally got her to talk to me.

I just wish she'd told me her first name, so I'd at least be able to find her phone number in the book. There were at least 200 Rollinses in there, and without a first name, I had nothing to go on without calling every single one of them.

I thought about her for the rest of the day, and when I laid my head down to go to sleep that night. I even dreamed of her. But for the rest of the weekend, I had my head wrapped up in the new season. By Monday morning, I had all but forgotten about my blond little angel.

"Mr. Donnelly," Julie said as I walked by her desk on my way into my office. I hadn't stopped, and she jumped up and was coming after me with her finger raised as if to get my attention.

"Can I help you with something, Julie?" I asked. "I have several interviews set up for you this week," she said. "Ten each day, starting today."

"Interviews for what?" I asked, "TV Guide, Time Magazine?" With sweeps season underway and the new lineup coming, I figured everyone would want to talk to me.

"Not quite," she said. "Your potential wives." She had a huge grin on her face as she said it.

"Oh yes," I said. How could I have forgotten? The wife interviews. I guess I didn't expect her to set them up so quickly. "Thanks, Julie," was all I could think of to say.

"I hope you find someone suitable, sir," she said as she turned around and went back to her desk.

I walked into my office and closed the door behind me, grateful that Julie was so secretive. No one would ever find out about the wife interviews from her. I made a mental note to give her a raise on her next paycheck.

I sat down behind my desk and started working on next season's lineup, when a flash of panic came over me. "Julie, can you come in here please," I said on the intercom.

Julie came rushing into my office with a hot coffee within minutes. "Here you go, Mr. Donnelly, just the way you like it." God, she was dependable.

"That's great, Julie. But that's not why I called you in here. The women that I'm interviewing, do they know..."

"Now, Mr. Donnelly, if they knew why they were being interviewed we'd have every single woman in the entire state, or the entire country for that matter, running in here trying to get her greedy little fingers on your money. Don't you worry about that. They think they're interviewing to be your personal assistant."

"Thank you, Julie. That's perfect. But isn't it a little bit deceptive?"

"Aw, sir, isn't a wife an assistant of sorts?" she said as she winked at me and smiled. "You're not being deceptive, you're just not giving out the whole job description yet."

I could always count on Julie to make me feel better. She was one hell of a secretary. If she hadn't already been married, I probably would have married her myself years ago.

"When's the first interview?" I asked, looking down at my watch.

"Oh goodness," she said. "She's probably here now. Hold on, and I'll check."

Damn, I thought. I was hoping for more time to get ready. Trying to impress a potential future wife was a lot different than trying to impress a casual fling. I ran my fingers through my hair and straightened my tie as Julie let the first one into my office.

Her name was Meg. She was stuffy and she made me feel old. I listened to her ramble on for twenty minutes about how she had been a personal assistant to the former CEO of Calhoun Broadcasting and how I could benefit from having her on board. I didn't want her on anything. I was bored.

Right after she left, the next one came hurdling into my office dropping papers everywhere. After I helped her pick them up she sat down and we talked. I couldn't help but wonder how a woman could be so beautiful and not have a single stimulating word to say.

If my whole week was going to be like this, I'd rather be working on the lineup. It was far more interesting than these boring women that Julie had lined up as potential brides.

When number three came walking in, I was terrified. She was very military, and told me about how she runs a tight ship. She had all kinds of great ideas about organization and order, but she wasn't someone I wanted running my life, and I certainly didn't want her in my bed.

When she left, I got up to stretch my legs. Julie was sitting at her desk, so I thought I'd go over and talk to her for a second. "What the hell?" I said.

"What do you mean?" she asked as she continued typing away on her computer.

I put my hand over her monitor. "What the hell are you sending to me? These women aren't potential wives. One was a drill sergeant and the rest are boring as hell. Is there at least someone on the list that I'll enjoy talking to?"

She looked up at me and smirked. "Mr. Donnelly, the kind of girl that makes a good wife isn't the same kind of girl that usually piques your curiosity. Big breasts and a nice ass don't exactly make someone marriage material."

"I didn't say that's what I was looking for. I said I wanted someone that was at least interesting to talk to." As much as I liked Julie, she certainly knew how to push my buttons.

"Look, you need someone who can take care of you, hence the drill sergeant. You also need someone who would make a good mother, which is the reason for the others. My choices are all carefully calculated. Trust the process, Mr. Donnelly, trust the process."

I shook my head and smiled. "Trust the process, huh," I said as I looked out the window. "I can't even imagine spending a night with any one of these women, let alone the rest of my life." Just then, I saw the blond from the bar and coffee shop running down the street.

"Julie, I have to run out for a minute," I said as I hurried toward the elevator.

"But Mr. Donnelly, your next interview will be here any minute. What do I tell her?"

"I don't care what you tell her. Tell her the position's been filled. Tell them all that," I said as I hurried along. When I got on the elevator, I pushed buttons frantically. I had to get down there. I had to catch her, to see her, to talk to her.

When I stepped out onto the street, I smiled as I saw her in the distance running along in her heels. She hadn't gotten very far. I chased after her, wishing I knew her first name. "Miss Rollins," I called to no avail. She didn't hear me, or at least she didn't turn around.

When I finally caught up to her, I grabbed her elbow. "Miss Rollins," I said out of breath.

She turned around and glared at me with an alarmed expression on her face. I hadn't meant to scare her. After pulling her arm back, she started walking again, picking up her pace as I followed her.

"Can I help you?" she said as she continued walking. I loved the way her heels clicked on the sidewalk.

"That depends," I said. "Can I take you to lunch?"

"No," she said as she kept on going. "I don't have time for idle chit chat. I'm a little busy right now."

"Look, I don't know what I ever did to you," I said. "The other day I fixed your nail and your shoe. If I said something that upset you, I'm sorry. All I want to do is talk to you."

She turned around sharply and glared at me. "Thank you for all that. But right now, if you don't mind, I'm a little busy." Then she spun around on her heels and started rushing down the street again.

"I just wanted to talk to you," I said as she walked away.

"Some of us have work to do," she said sharply as she marched on down the street.

I turned around and walked back toward my office building, passing several other women on the way. *Why didn't any of them hold the same appeal for me?* I tried to feel some sort of attraction to any of them, but none of them could hold a candle to her. She still wouldn't give me the time of day, but I was more determined than ever to win her over.

"What was that all about?" Julie asked when I got back to the office.

"Nothing. I just remembered that I needed something, so I ran out to get it," I said as I grabbed a coffee.

"Are you ready to resume the interviews then?" she asked as she looked down at her computer screen.

"No. I meant what I said about that. Who wants to marry a billionaire is now officially over. Finding a wife and mother to bear my children is something I'm going to have to do on my own," I said, looking up at the ceiling. I didn't think I'd be able to find anyone in a million years. No one would put up with my antics. But I was sure as hell going to try.

Chapter 6 ~ Jerrica

I WALKED THROUGH THE door of my apartment, exhausted from my first day on the job. After grabbing a yogurt out of the fridge, I slipped off my heels and sat down on the couch to relax while I stared out the window and reflected on my day.

"You're home already," Liz said as she came down the hall. "How was the first day at the new job?"

"Great, terrible, and everything in between. Right now, I'm basically a gopher. It's not what I thought it was at all. I thought I'd be doing the real work. Instead they have me running all over the city picking up supplies and delivering things," I said as I rubbed my aching feet.

"Awww, it will get better. Do you want a glass of wine?" she asked as she poured one for herself.

"No. I better not. I have to go in early tomorrow, lucky me."

"It was only your first day. I'm sure after you prove yourself they'll give you actual projects to work on. Give it a few weeks. If you still hate it, you can always start applying for other jobs. Just don't let it get you down."

"It's not really that bad. I'm just disappointed, you know. I wanted to jump right in and get right into the swing of things. I'm going to try to stick it out and work my way up the ladder."

"Good for you. That's the spirit," she said as she patted me on the back. "Oh, guess what? I have a date on Saturday."

"With who?" I asked her suspiciously. Liz didn't date. She fell in love a lot, but her idea of dating was hanging out with some-one watching movies on the couch or eating takeout. For her to use the word "date" meant the guy must be special.

"With Jimmy Calhoun," she said as she scrunched up her face.

"Jimmy Calhoun? From high school, how the hell did that happen?"

"I ran into him at the supermarket the other day. He's a lawyer now and recently divorced. We got talking and one thing led to another, and yeah, he's taking me to dinner."

"Wow, that's awesome," I said as I nudged her shoulder. "Congratulations. I hope it all works out."

"It's just a date," she said. "I'm trying not to read too much into it. How about you, anything new and exciting going on in your life?"

"No. Well, do you remember that guy from the bar on Friday night?"

"Yeah, yeah, the one who thought he could buy us with a drink. What about him?" she asked as she stared at me intently, waiting for the gossip.

"Remember when I went shopping the next day?"

"Yeah, yeah, keep going," she said impatiently.

"Well, I ran into him again at a coffee shop."

"And...please tell me there's more," she said with her hand on her hip.

"I had broken a nail and he fixed it for me with super glue, and then he fixed my shoe."

"Go on..."

"Well, I ran into him again today. I was running errands for work and he tried to stop me on the street."

"What did he want?"

"He asked to take me to lunch. But of course I told him I was too busy. I have too much on the go right now to get bogged down with a relationship."

"Oh, so you're attracted to him," she said with a glint of sarcasm in her voice.

"I never said that," I said.

"Yes, you did. You said you were too busy for a relationship."

"So?"

"If you didn't like him, you would have said you weren't interested in him, or you didn't like him."

"Well, I don't like how he assumes that I'm interested, or the way he tries to demand my time," I said as I pondered on the idea.

"But you are attracted to him," she said, smiling at me mischievously.

"Well, he does have a nice smile, and a killer butt. Oh, and his eyes, the way his eyes sparkle in the sunlight..."

"Jerrica, just admit it, you're smitten."

The next morning when I was getting ready for work, I kept thinking about my conversation with Liz the night before. *Maybe I do like him,* I thought. It wasn't that hard to believe that I could be smitten with him. After all, he certainly was charming.

I tried to put him out of my mind while I finished getting ready and hurried to the office. If I was going to move up the ladder, I had a lot of work to do. My career was very important to me, and I didn't have time to sit around daydreaming about him.

"Jerrica, I'm glad you're here," my boss said. "Can you run over to CHI and grab a copy of the dailies?"

"That's what I'm here for," I said as I grabbed my purse, ready to head back out the door. I hurried along the streets determined to make it back in record time. If running errands was what it took to get a promotion, I'd be the best damn gopher they ever had.

I was hurrying along so fast, that I didn't even look up to see the gentleman in the grey suit that was walking toward me until I bumped into him with a *thud*. "Miss Rollins," he said. "We meet again."

I sighed in disbelief as I realized who he was. "Yes, I'll go to lunch with you," I said.

"I don't remember asking," he laughed. "But it was nice running into you, or rather it was nice being run into by you."

I felt my face turning crimson. What an ass, I thought. "Oh, I... I... I'm sorry," I stammered. I wanted to cry, and I knew I had to get out of there fast. I nodded my head and started to walk away.

"Miss Rollins," he said as he grabbed my elbow. "The restaurant on the corner at noon?"

"I'll be there," I said, smiling. Then I put my head down and walked away. I felt like such a klutz for walking into him like that, and an even bigger idiot for assuming he was going to ask me out again. At least he decided to humor me by giving me a pity date.

As the morning wore on, I wished I knew his last name or his phone number so I could cancel our lunch date. I really didn't want to get into anything right now, and if it was just a pity date, I could do without it.

When eleven forty-five rolled around, I could feel my stomach tying in knots. I was getting so nervous as I stared at the clock. I started getting myself primped up to head out. Just because I went to lunch with him, didn't mean I had to actually date him.

"Table for one?" the maître d' asked.

"No, I'm meeting someone," I said. "Jason... I don't know his last name, but his first name is Jason."

"You must be Miss Rollins," the host said. "Right this way." He showed me to a little table tucked in a far-off corner where Jason sat waiting for me. As soon as he saw me, he stood up and reached out his hand to take mine.

"Miss Rollins," he said. "I'm so glad you could make it. Won't you join me?"

"Please call me Jerrica," I said. In the beginning I loved making him call me Miss Rollins, but now it seemed so formal.

"So tell me, Jerrica, what do you do?" he asked as he read over the menu.

"I'm a PR intern at Donnelly Multimedia," I said as I played with my napkin.

"I see," he said with a surprised expression on his face.

"Does that surprise you?" I asked.

"I just pictured you as working in banking and finance," he said quickly.

"What do you do, Jason?" I asked.

"I work at a large corporation. A lot of administration crap, really boring stuff. Now tell me, do you like your job?"

"Right now, not so much. I'm new, so I don't get to do anything exciting. I'm determined, though. I'm going to work my way up in the company as quickly as I can."

"Good for you," he said. "Now tell me this, Jerrica, can you read a word of that menu?"

"Not really," I laughed.

"Why don't you let me order for you then?" he said as he reached across the table and took my hand in his.

"Okay," I agreed. When the waiter came over I listened in awe as he ordered for us in French. "Where did you learn that?" I asked.

"Oh, that. I went to a French Immersion school," he said. "Now tell me about your family."

"I have two sisters, both older than me and both live out of state. What about you, do you have any brothers or sisters?"

"One brother, one sister. What about your parents?"

"Do you get along with your brother and sister?" I asked.

"We get along fine. Tell me about your parents." I knew there was no getting around answering the question. "My parents live in Oklahoma," I said. I didn't think there was any need to tell him more at that point. "What about your parents?"

"Do you get along with your parents?" he asked.

"Yes," I lied. I hadn't talked to my parents in four years, not that it was any of his business. "Now, tell me about your parents."

"They're fine," he said as the waiter brought our food to the table.

"Guess what?" I yelled as I ran into the apartment after work.

Liz ran to the door with her arms out-stretched. "You got a raise?"

"No, I went to lunch with the guy."

"And?"

I told her all about our lunch date. As she and I analyzed the whole thing, I started to think it was weird that he had me talking about my job, myself, and my family, while he barely revealed a thing about himself.

"So, are you going to see him again?" she asked.

"Saturday night," I said, smiling. "He's taking me to dinner."

63

AFTER OUR LUNCH DATE, I hurried back to my office. *Goddammit, how could the girl of my dreams be one of my own employees?* I thought. When she said Donnelly Multimedia, I thought I was going to have a heart attack.

"Julie," I said into my intercom, "can you come in here for a moment?"

"What is it, Jason?" she said as she hurried into my office with a coffee.

"I need you to take care of a little problem for me."

"What is it this time, Jason?" she asked, shaking her head.

"Jerrica Rollins in PR."

"Jason, not again. Seriously, you've got to stop..."

"Just listen to me for two minutes." I told her what I wanted her to do, and she shook her head as she got up to walk out of my office. "I'll do it this time, but from there on in you're on your own."

On Saturday night I met Jerrica at her apartment building to take her to dinner. I considered sending a driver to get her, but I didn't want her to know I had money yet. I figured that was a secret better left kept for as long as possible.

Once they found out you had money, they started hinting about financial problems, or started falling in love quick. The next thing you knew they wanted to move in with you. If she was the one that would settle me down and bear my children, I wanted it to happen because she loved me, and not my bank book.

"Hey Jason," she said as she stepped out of the building. She looked so beautiful in her black silk dress that cut off mid-thigh.

"Well, hello, Miss Rollins," I said as I took her hand and kissed her on the cheek. "You're looking quite stunning this evening, I must say."

"You look pretty good yourself," she said as she smiled up at me. I was glad she noticed. I had worked hard at looking dressed up enough for the evening, but no so dressed up that I looked wealthy. I almost felt naked without a jacket and tie.

After dinner, she talked me into going to a dance bar of all things. When we walked through the doors, I felt like the oldest man in the place, but she immediately made me feel like a teenager again.

"Let's go dance," she said as she grabbed my hand and pulled me toward the dance floor. The fog and laser lights added to the illusion. They reminded me so much of the strobe lights from my younger days.

After we hung around there for a while, we decided to go for a moonlit stroll. She was stumbling around on her heels, even though she'd only had a couple of drinks.

Taking pity on her aching feet, I picked her up and carried her back to my car.

When we got to her apartment building, I offered to help her inside. "No," she said. "I know what you want, and dinner and a few drinks isn't getting it."

"Miss Rollins, Jerrica, all I want is to see that you get inside without landing on your ass."

She said she was fine as she fell out of the car onto the sidewalk. I helped her up and walked her inside the building and straight to her door.

"Goodnight," I said as I turned around to walk away.

"Aren't you going to kiss me good-night?" she asked as she pouted.

"I didn't think dinner and a few drinks could buy that," I said with a grin.

"Get back here," she said as she pulled on my arm. I practically flew back to her and took her in my arms, while I kissed her goodnight.

Chapter 8 ~ Jerrica

THE MONDAY AFTER MY dinner date with Jason, I got called into my supervisor's office. I thought for sure I was getting fired, and I couldn't figure out what I had done wrong. My eyes stung with tears, and I kicked myself for not having thicker skin.

I sat in the hot seat and waited for Mr. Rompwell, my supervisor, to come in. He'd called me for the meeting, the least he could do was be on time. The longer I waited the more nervous I became.

Finally, I heard the door handle turn. My pulse started rising when I realized the end was near. I braced myself for what I knew was coming.

"Miss Rollins," he said. "We've decided to promote you. Starting today, you'll be an associate PR in new series development."

"I don't understand. How does that work?"

"You'll be handling public relations for new series that we produce, the stars, the shows, that sort of thing."

"Are you serious?" I asked him, almost jumping out of my chair. I wanted to hug that man, I was so excited.

"Yes, I am. There's an office waiting for you up on the third floor. Now pack your things and go."

I couldn't believe it. One week on the job, and I got a major promotion. My resume must have really blown them away even though it only had the projects I worked on in college on it. I couldn't wait to get home and tell Liz, and more importantly, I couldn't wait to tell Jason.

I gathered my desk up quickly, and made my way to the third floor to claim my office. I was almost afraid that if I took too long they'd realize that they made a mistake and change their minds.

After spending the day getting up to speed on my new position, I raced home from work. "Liz," I yelled when I threw open the door of the apartment. "I got a promotion."

"Yay," she said. "Tell me all about it."

"I can't right now because Jason's coming to pick me up in a few minutes. But I'm now an Associate PR in new series. Basically I handle PR for new series and the people who star in them," I said as I ran my fingers through my hair.

"Good for you," she said. "See, I told you that it would get better."

The buzzer rang. "Well, I better go," I said as I raced out the door to go meet Jason. When I told him about the promotion, he gave me a pleased smile.

"I think that calls for a celebration," he said. "What do you say we go for dinner?"

Over the next few weeks Jason and I had a whirlwind relationship. We were practically inseparable when we weren't working. I knew I was falling in love with him whether I had time for it or not.

One Friday night when Liz was out of town visiting her parents, he walked me up to my apartment like he always did. It was still early, so I invited him in for a drink. We sat on the sofa while we talked and laughed in between kisses for hours.

When things really started to get heated up, he started unbuttoning my blouse. "I think you should go now," I said. "It's getting late, and I'm getting tired." I pushed his hands away and buttoned my blouse back up.

Jason's eyes narrowed. "We've been dating for weeks now, Jerrica, and I haven't even gotten to second base. What's up with that?"

"I'm sorry Jason, it's just not the right time yet. When something happens between us, I want to make sure everything's perfect."

"I thought everything was fucking perfect tonight," he said as he stormed out the door.

As soon as he left I burst into tears. *Maybe I should have just slept with him,* I thought. But I was a believer in the old adage, sex too fast, it won't last. Ten minutes later my phone rang. It was Jason. I tried to compose myself before I answered.

"Hello," I said.

"Jerrica, I'm so sorry," he said into the phone.

"Look, Jason. I get it. I totally do. You're a guy and you have needs. I'll tell you what. You swing that car around right now, and

I'll fuck you right here, right now. In fact, I'll start ripping my clothes off while you're on your way. I just want you to tell me one thing first. When's my birthday, Jason?"

He was silent on the other end.

"You don't know, do you? I'll give you another chance. What's my favorite color?"

He was still silent.

"That's exactly my point. We don't know each other. Before I get intimate with you, I want to know everything about you and your life. I want us to know everything there is to know about each other. I don't want to just jump into something blindly. I want to fall in love."

As soon as I said the last sentence, I wished I hadn't. I'd put it all out there on the table and there was no taking it back.

"That's what I want too, Jerrica," he said. "I'm so sorry for my behavior tonight. We'll take it as slow as you want. But just so you know, my birthday is April 21st, and my favorite color is blue. If there's anything else you want to know, just ask."

My heart melted when he said it. I wished there were some way I could reach through the phone and wrap my arms around him.

"My birthday is March 24th and my favorite color is purple," I said.

"Can I come back over?" he asked.

"Jason..."

"I was just kidding," he said. "I do want to get to know you, Jerrica. You have no idea how much you mean to me."

Chapter 9 ~ Jason

THAT WOMAN WOULD DRIVE me crazy if I let her. She filled both my mind and my dreams. No matter how hard I tried, I couldn't stop thinking about her. In all my life, not one other woman had bewitched me quite the way she had.

As much as it frustrated me that she wouldn't jump into bed with me, it made my feelings for her grow even stronger. If I thought she was the perfect bride for me and mother for my heir before, her willpower confirmed it.

We spent the next few days concentrating on getting to know each other better. Every date was like 20 questions with kisses for rewards. I felt like I knew everything about her, and the more I knew, the more I loved, and the more I wanted to know.

Then one night it happened. I knew that eventually it would, and in fact, I was surprised that it happened sooner. She asked me my last name. "Donnelly," I said as I stared her straight in the eyes. I was expecting her to start asking questions about the company and about my parentage, but she didn't. She didn't even connect my last name with the company she worked for.

I let it go. She asked a question and I gave her an honest answer. She didn't go any further into it, so neither did I. It wasn't exactly lying, it was just leaving part of the truth out. Plus, I enjoyed pretending to be a normal person around her.

Then I ran into another problem. "So," she said one afternoon. "You've been to my place a few times now, and I've never seen yours."

Oh God, I thought. "Well, in that case, why don't I cook you dinner on Saturday night?" I said it before I even realized the mess I was getting myself into. I couldn't let her see my house without giving myself away.

The next morning when I went into work, I stopped off at Julie's desk. "I need another favor," I said, giving her my best smile and puppy dog eyes.

"What is it this time?" she said as she looked up from her computer screen.

"I need you to rent me a standard apartment before the weekend, and have it furnished." I rested my hand on her desk and tried to sound as casual as possible.

"Are you kidding? Jason, that's impossible. Friday is three days away. How on earth do you expect me to furnish an apartment in that amount of time, and why do you need it in the first place?"

"I don't know, call IKEA or whatever that place is called. There's this girl..."

"Oh, there we go. Let me guess, Miss Rollins. I still don't understand why you need the apartment, though."

"She wants to see my house. I've been to her place a few times but she's never been to mine. If she comes to my house, she'll know I have money."

"Jason, you've been seeing her for weeks now. Just how long do you plan on keeping this from her? I could understand you being secretive in the beginning, but this is bordering on ridiculous. If she still likes you despite your idiosyncrasies, she'd love you whether you owned the city, or didn't have a penny."

I put my hands in my pockets and looked at the floor, almost embarrassed by my shenanigans. "I know," I said. "But I'm not ready for her to know yet. I want the time to be right, and it just doesn't feel right yet."

"Okay, how big of an apartment do you want?" she asked. I could tell she felt sorry for me. It was also obvious that part of her couldn't possibly understand my problems.

"I have no idea," I laughed. "The normal size, I guess." I walked into my office and sat down at my desk. Now that I had the apartment, I just had to figure out how to cook.

By the time Saturday rolled around, I'd already burnt the hell out of several recipes and knew there was no way I'd be able to pull off a dinner fit for Jerrica. I decided my best bet was to order takeout, and put it in a pan before she arrived. That way I could pretend I spent all day cooking it just for her.

After telling her where I "lived," I asked her to come by at around six thirty p.m. I spent the afternoon getting myself ready. At five thirty p.m. I picked up our dinners, and at six o'clock p.m. I unlocked the door to my apartment for the first time.

Everything was running exactly according to schedule. I hung my jacket in the front closet, and then went to work in the kitchen. After I put the wine in the fridge to chill, I reached through the cupboards until I found pans that I thought would work.

Julie had done a great job of setting the apartment up. I made a mental note to give her another raise as I put our dinner on the stove. At six thirty p.m. on the dot, a knock came to the door. I rolled my sleeves up, and splashed some water on my forehead to make it look like I'd been sweating in the kitchen all afternoon.

"Welcome to my humble abode," I said as I opened the door for her. She wore a blue dress that was absolutely stunning the way it changed color in the light.

"You have a lovely apartment," she said as she came in and looked around. "It's very clean."

"I just cleaned up today," I said, thinking fast. "I'm actually a slob."

"Then you won't mind if I do this," she said as she grabbed a throw pillow off the couch and tossed it across the room.

"Nope." I really didn't care. It wasn't really my house, but she didn't know that.

"So, are you going to take me on the grand tour?" I kept trying to concentrate on dinner, but she was eager to look around. I knew I should have gone to the apartment earlier so I'd have time to check it out. *Oh well,* I thought. *It's just an apartment. How hard can it be?*

"Yeah, sure. For starters, you're standing in my living room/dining room, and I'm standing in the kitchen. If you follow me, I'll show you the rest of my castle." I took her down the narrow hall. "To our left, we have the bathroom," I said as I opened the door to a huge linen closet full of towels.

"Wow, you wouldn't want to make that mistake in the middle of the night," she laughed.

"I'm sorry. I'm just so nervous about cooking for you," I said as I shook my head. "Over here is where I sleep every night and dream of you." I almost died on the spot when I opened the door and realized it was the bathroom.

"Good to know." She nodded her head. "Let me guess, this room is your bedroom," she said as she opened the last door.

"Yes, yes, that's the one." I walked in with her and sat down on the four-poster bed in the middle of the room. "Do you know why four-poster beds exist?"

"Because they're beautiful and add character to a room?"

"No. In the middle ages, they had thatch roofs, and they leaked and bugs got in. The four posts and canopies kept the bugs and dirt from getting on the bedding."

"I see," she said as she looked around the room at the pictures that hung on the walls.

I couldn't believe I just tried to make a conversation with her about dirty beds and bugs. All I wanted to do was get back to the kitchen, feed her, and then take her out. I wasn't in my element in this apartment.

"The one thing I find interesting is that nothing in this apartment seems personal," she said. "You told me blue was your favorite color, but you don't have anything blue. You have all sorts of pictures on the wall, but no pictures of your family."

As I tried to think of a quick explanation, the smoke detector started going off in the kitchen. We ran out there, and I started scrambling through cupboards looking for a fire extinguisher while our dinner burned to a crisp.

She walked over and turned the burners off. "Where's your fire extinguisher?"

"I don't know." I kept rummaging through the cupboards.

"Do you have any baking soda? That will work too."

"I don't know," I growled. "I'm sorry, I just need to put out the fire for now."

"Okay, hand me a lid."

I looked at her like I didn't have a clue because I didn't. She started going through cupboards herself, and found a lid to smother the flames. I watched in amazement as the fire died out.

"We need to talk," I said as I led her over to the couch and sat down beside her. I could tell by the look on her face she thought I was going to break up with her.

The end of Billionaire Seeks an Heir Book 1: Unplanned Fairy Tale

To find out what happens next: Read Book 2 – Unraveled Lives

Thanks for Reading!

Thank you for purchasing my book. It's that sort of support that allows me to continue doing something that I love every day. If you liked the read, please consider leaving a review so more people can find and enjoy it too!

Want More of Misha's books? Join Misha's Newsletter and you'll always be notified about new releases ~

www.mishacarver.com/newsletter

About the Author

I love to write stories about powerful men and women and the romances fiascos they find themselves in. Whether it's billionaires, shifters, bad boys, or just ordinary people, they'll make their way into one of my books.

So many stories flood my imagination every day. I love to write them down so other people can enjoy them too. For me writing isn't a job. When I write, I see the stories playing out in my head. It's almost like going to the movies for free. I hope you have the same experience when you read them.

Also By Misha Carver

Shifter/Paranormal Romances

Purrfect Mates Series

Purrfect Chaos (Book 1)

Purrfect Storm (Book 2)

Purrfect Harmony (Book 3)

Purrfect Mates Box Set

Contemporary/New Adult Romances

Billionaire Seeks An Heir Series

Unplanned Fairy Tale (Book 1)

Unraveled Lives (Book 2)

Unforgettable Melody (Book 3)

Billionaire Seeks An Heir Boxed Set
Collection

Big City Heat Firefighter Series

Light My Fire (Book 1)

I'm On Fire (Book 2)

Ring of Fire (Book 3)

Sasha's Storm – (steamy menage romance)

Second Chance Christmas Romances

The Christmas Homecoming (Book 1)

The Christmas Reunion (Book 2)

The Christmas Spirit (Book 3)

Jingle Bell Shifters

Jingle Bell Growl (Book 1)

Jingle Bell Howl (Book 2)

Jingle Bell Prowl (Book 3)